Let's Connect!

Thank you so much for taking the time to read this story. It's one of many and I pray that it will bless and inspire you in some way! I would love to hear your positive feedback as well as your constructive criticism on this story so that I can continue to grow and develop in my skill as a writer and author! When you have time, please contact me and/or provide your feedback at one of the links below! God bless and thank you in advance for your love, continued prayers and support.

Sincerely,
Author Aundrya Schnel

www.authoraundryaschnel.weebly.com
www.facebook.com/writeronamission
*Instagram: @writer.on.a.mission

****PLEASE POST A REVIEW ON AMAZON!!****
YOUR REVIEWS MEAN EVERYTHING!!

I dedicate this story to the men and women (*young and old*) who have experienced any form of abuse or manipulation at the hands of a pastor or leadership in the church! Time out for calling this *"church hurt"* and making those victimized out to be the bad guy for the sake of *"covering their pastor"*! What we are witnessing today in the pulpits is not how the true church was ever established and until leadership repent and turn from their wicked, unbiblical and manipulative tactics, there will continue to be a great falling away from the faith...

God Bless,
Author Aundrya Schnel

"The church is the only place where you can get robbed and nobody calls the police!"
~LeAndria Johnson

"The person who didn't get picked for kickball, can become pastor..."
~Sharde Martin

Jeremiah 5:26-29 (MSG)
"My people are infiltrated by wicked men,
unscrupulous men on the hunt. They set traps for the
unsuspecting. Their victims are innocent men and
women. Their houses are stuffed with ill-gotten gain,
like a hunter's bag full of birds. Pretentious and
powerful and rich, hugely obese, oil with rolls of fat.
Worse, they have no conscience. Right and wrong
mean nothing to them. They stand for nothing, stand
up for no one, throw orphans to the wolves, exploit the
poor. Do you think I'll stand by and do nothing about
this? God's decree. Do you think I'll take serious
measures against a people like this?"

Jeremiah 6:13-15 (MSG)
"Everyone's after the dishonest dollar, little people and
big people alike. Prophets and priests and everyone in
between twist words and doctor truth. My people are
broken--shattered and they put on Band-Aids, saying
"It's not so bad, you'll be just fine." But things are not
"just fine"! Do you suppose they are embarrassed by
this outrage? No, they have no shame. They don't even
know how to blush. There's no hope for them. They've
hit bottom and there's no getting up. As far as I'm
concerned, they're finished. God has spoken..."

INTRODUCTION

"I am so proud of you!"

"Thanks Mama, I appreciate it..."

"Are you okay?"

"Yes ma'am, I just wished things were different..."

"I know you do and I'm sorry things didn't go as planned..."

"It wasn't your fault, but thank you..."

"Are you sure you guys can handle being at this university knowing you won't be able to play?"

"Yes ma'am, we'll work through it. We both really wanted to go to school there..."

"Okay, I understand. I love you!"

"I love you too, Mama!"

"Do you remember my number one rule for when you get to school?"

"Yes Mama, you don't want me to step foot in my uncle's church!"

"That's right and I need you to follow that rule no matter what happens, no matter what he says! Do you understand?"

"Yes ma'am, I got it. I won't go. It's not like we ever went to church anyway out here!"

"I know but my brother has a way with words and I won't be surprised if he or one of your cousins don't approach you guys about coming."

"I understand but don't worry Mama, we're not checking for church like that anyway."

"Okay, good..."

"Can I ask you something?"

"What's that?"
"Not that it's a big deal but I always wondered why you and Aunt Tracy never took us to church. I mean you guys are preacher's kids and all of our uncles are involved in church but you guys are not."
"I wondered when this would come up..."
"Oh, did I say something wrong Mama?"
"No, you're not wrong but it's complicated and one day you and I will talk about that..."
"Okay..."
"In the meantime, just know that there is a reason your Aunt Tracy and I want nothing to do with the church and there's a reason why we've never taken you to any of your uncle's churches..."
"I understand. But we've always prayed and believed in God though..."
"That's right, always! You don't need a church building to do that and don't ever forget it..."
"Yes ma'am, I won't. Awe man Mama, you got me curious now. I want to know this big secret about our uncles' church..."
"Don't worry sweetheart, you will know soon enough. There will be a breaking of day and at that point, the light will shine on all the dark things that have been covered up with religion all these years!"
"What do you mean by that, Mama?"
"Just give it time and you will see..."

FOR MY PASTOR X
Break of Day

Jamaal Day is a freshman at the University of Florida (UF) in Gainesville, Florida. He was born and raised in Miami where he grew up with his mother, Katrina Day and his four younger brothers; Antoine, Mario, Keon and Brandon. Without having his father in his life and being kept away from the men in his family, Jamaal never knew what it was like to have male role models in his life to guide him. But Katrina did her best to raise him to be successful and she never fell short in holding him accountable and making sure he stayed on top of his classes in school. She worked two and even three jobs at times to make sure he and his brothers had the best education and were able to participate in extracurricular activities so they wouldn't be distracted by other young men in their neighborhood who dealt drugs.

All of the hard work had seemed to pay off Jamaal's senior year of high school when he was accepted into college at UF on a full ride basketball scholarship. Jamaal and his family were excited and were certain that nothing would stand in the way of his bright future. That was until a month after basketball season ended when Jamaal and his best friend, Ramon were both injured severely in a car accident with a drunk driver who ran the light. The unfortunate accident tragically ended the lives of two of their teammates who were in the car with them the night the accident took place. Jamaal and Ramon survived but spent several weeks after their release from the hospital going through physical therapy to regain strength in their arms and legs. The unfortunate accident prevented them from ever being able to run full speed again and play sports. Ultimately they both lost their scholarship leaving them to pay for college with financial aid and other qualifying scholarships.

Jamaal was initially going to take his mother's advice when she told him to reconsider going to UF by choosing a school that didn't cost as much for tuition. But when Ramon decided that he wanted to attend UF even though he would not have his basketball scholarship, Jamaal decided to go with him so they could maintain their dream to attend college together. Jamaal is now 19-years-old and is approaching the start of his second semester at UF after managing to make the Dean's List his first semester. But with the cost for tuition, Jamaal's financial aid and scholarship money wasn't enough to cover all of his expenses so he and Ramon both worked part-time for one of the local restaurants on campus to make extra money.

To Jamaal's surprise, none of his cousins, uncles and other relatives who live in the area tried talking to him except for his older cousin, Earnest who is a junior and plays on the UF basketball team. Some days it's hard for Jamaal to see his cousin playing on the team he was supposed to be a part of but he does his best to accept things for what they are and remain grateful that he and his best friend survived the crash. Earnest's girlfriend, Dana has her own apartment off campus and she's a great cook. So when Jamaal and Ramon get tired of takeout and fast food, she and Earnest always invite them over for a home cooked meal.

It's the week before the semester starts and Jamaal was looking forward to being off for the entire week with Ramon before going back to work and another full course load. After going to the movies, Jamaal and Ramon went to a local restaurant nearby that a lot of the other students gathered at to eat food, watch sports and engage in other activities that are offered. As Jamaal and Ramon sit outside talking and finishing up their food, they are approached by two of Jamaal's cousins, Calvin Day, Jr. and Preston Day who both attend UF as well.

"What's up Cousin! I was hoping we would run into each other at some point!" Calvin said as he and Preston slapped hands with him.
"Hey guys. You know I've been on campus since right before fall semester right? You expect me to believe you didn't know I was here?" Jamaal asked as they both laughed a little.
"C'mon man, we knew you were here. We just had to wait for the right time to approach you with Earnest on our backs and ready to report to your mom and Aunt Tracy if he sees us talking to you." Preston replied as Jamaal's expression changed.
"Wait a minute, you're saying Earnest told you not to talk to me?" Jamaal asked.
"Yeah, he did. He didn't tell you?" Preston asked.
"He asked me a couple of times I talked to you guys and I told him I hadn't but he never told me he did all of that." Jamaal replied.

"Well, I'm sure you already know why that is right?" Calvin asked as Jamaal nodded.

"Yeah, I've already been lectured by my mom, Aunt Tracy and Earnest. Wait, let me introduce you to my best friend. Guys, this is Ramon. Ramon, these are two more of my cousins, Calvin and Preston Day." Jamaal said as they slapped hands with him.

"It's nice to meet you." Ramon said.

"It's nice to meet you too, Ramon. We were really sorry to hear about your accident but we're glad you're both still alive after what happened." Calvin said.

"Yes and we definitely offer our condolences to your friends' families who passed too." Preston replied as Jamaal and Ramon nodded.

"Thanks, we appreciate it. I know our families don't talk like that but I thought I would have seen you guys at some point when I was in the hospital." Jamaal said as Calvin and Preston glanced at each other.

"Jamaal, we're sorry about that. If we could have come, we would have. I promise. We asked Earnest about your condition every day." Calvin said.

"Dang, so the beef between our family is so real that you can't even come to the hospital to see me when I'm hurt? What if I would have been one of the guys who died? You wouldn't have been able to come to the funeral either?" Jamaal asked, surprised.

"I hate to say it Jamaal but with Aunt Katrina and Aunt Tracy shielding you and the rest of our cousins the way they do, they would have kept us away no matter what." Preston told them.

"Jamaal, you seem way too surprised about all of this. I know your mom has talked to you by now right?" Calvin asked.

"Not really. I mean, I asked her what the deal was and she kept saying I would know the truth soon enough. But she still made it clear that she wanted me to stay away from Uncle Walter's church, which is fine. We were never churchgoers anyway." Jamaal said.

"What about you Ramon? You want to visit us sometime?" Calvin asked.

"Oh no, I'm good. If he's not going, I'm not going." Ramon replied.

"I know money has to be tight right now since you weren't able to keep that basketball scholarship. Am I right?" Preston asked.

"Yeah it is sometimes but we manage and Earnest helps us out when he can too." Jamaal said.

"Earnest may be on scholarship but we know he doesn't have money like that to help you out so what are you doing for extra money?" Calvin asked.

"We work part-time on campus." Jamaal said.

"Are you serious? Those campus jobs only pay minimum wage! The tuition can't be paid with that chump change!" Preston said.

"I get it but we can't be picky so we do what we have to do." Jamaal said.

"We totally understand Jamaal and when we were freshman, we were in a similar situation with our money. But our problem got solved and it didn't take very long." Calvin said.

"Guys, don't try and play me! Both of your dads are loaded so what money troubles could you have possibly been having?" Jamaal asked.

"Yeah, our folks may be loaded but we learned at an early age that we have to earn our keep and no silver spoon has ever been handed to us." Calvin replied.

"Our parents got us our cars when we graduated but after that, we had to work for what we got and now we're making money in our sleep and we're both about to graduate this spring with our money sitting real high." Preston told them as he and Calvin slapped hands.

"Okay, good for you! Why are you telling us this?" Jamaal asked.

"Oh shoot, there's Myra! Bro, I'll be back! Nice to meet you guys!" Ramon said as he quickly grabbed his phone and ran to catch up to her as she walked with her friends.

"Oh wow, he goes with Myra?" Preston asked.

"Not officially but he's working on it any chance he gets. Listen, why are you telling me about how much money you have?" Jamaal asked as Preston and Calvin sat across from him.

"We're telling you because we can help you make the same, maybe more and you won't need that job to pay for school. Are you interested?" Preston asked as Jamaal paused and thought for a moment before responding.

"I guess that depends on what I would be doing." Jamaal replied.

"Uncle Walter has a business that he does on the side when he's not pastoring and it's set up for college students to make the money they need to cover expenses that scholarships and financial aid can't cover." Calvin said.

"Really? Earnest never mentioned that to me. Has he ever done it?" Jamaal asked.

"Well he never chose to get on board but it was offered to him." Calvin told him as Jamaal's expression changed.

"Okay, I don't understand. Earnest had the chance to make extra money to cover expenses for school and he turned it down? Why would he do that? He tells me all the time how tight money is for him." Jamaal replied, confused by Calvin and Preston's response.

"See, this is why we like you! You're smart and you're always thinking. There was a small catch to all of this and it involved membership at the church. Like you, Earnest refused based on all the things Aunt Tracy has filled his head with about our family and about Uncle Walter's church." Preston said as Jamaal nodded.

"I should have known. So this offer you're trying to make me can only happen if I join Uncle Walter's church?" Jamaal asked.

"Yeah, it's somewhat of a members only thing so that's why." Preston replied.

"Okay, I get that for anyone else who wants in but I'm family. Uncle Walter can't make an exception?" Jamaal replied.

"No, he's not going to do that. If he was, Earnest would not have turned down the offer. Listen Jamaal, we know Aunt Katrina told you to stay away from us and the church but you're a grown man now! How about for once you check things out for yourself and if you like it, you can stay. If it doesn't work for you, then you can go." Calvin said.

"He's right, Jamaal! Be your own man and make your own decision. What do you really have to lose at this point? Is your mom paying your way to be going to school here right now?" Preston asked.

"No, she's not. She tries to help when she can but she can't always do it because she has my brothers to take care of too." Jamaal said.

"Okay man, that's fine. That's sort of what happens when you're the oldest and there's younger siblings who can't pull their own weight yet." Preston said.

"Yeah, that's true..."

"Alright then, so are you in? Do you want to come to the church so we can get you into this business?" Calvin asked.

"It's tempting but guys, I still don't know. I mean for one, you still haven't told me what it is Uncle Walter has you doing. On top of that, Earnest will tell my mom if he sees that I'm coming to Uncle Walter's church with you guys!" Jamaal replied.

"Jamaal, if you're discrete about it and don't be obvious about anything; he'll never know. Besides, we can have a little talk with him to make sure he doesn't say anything in the event he does find out." Preston told him.

"What about my mom, my brothers and Aunt Tracy come to visit the campus? They're going to know something is up." Jamaal said.

"Listen, you tell us when they're coming and we won't come around and you stay away from the church until they leave. They won't know anything if we do it that way." Calvin said.

"So what do you guys do?" Jamaal asked as Preston and Calvin glanced at each other again.

"We basically sell products and services to clients and make profit off the number of items we get them to purchase." Calvin said as Jamaal nodded.

"You mean items made by the church like shirts, cups and stuff like that?" Jamaal asked.

"Right, it's like that. Listen, I hope you're in after asking us all these questions." Preston said as Jamaal laughed a little.

"I think I want to do it. Can you get Ramon in too?" Jamaal asked as Preston and Calvin glanced at Ramon who was still talking to Myra next to her car.

"Sure, he can get in if he's willing to join the church. Just make sure he uses the same discretion you plan to use so Earnest, your mom and Aunt Tracy don't find out." Preston told him.

"Oh yeah, don't worry about that. I will. I'll talk to him about it first and see what he says. So if I'm ready, I would come to church on Sunday right?" Jamaal asked as Preston pulled out two cards and handed it to him.

"The information for the meeting location is on the card. The other card is the church info." Preston said.

"The business is called Time of Day?" Jamaal asked, looking at the card.

"Right, that's it. If you're serious about starting, you would meet us there at eight on Friday. That's when we talk to the new hires and lay everything out for them." Preston replied as Jamaal nodded.

"We do it every Friday so if you don't decide this week because you need time to think, that is okay. But there's thousands of dollars with your name on it and the sooner you say yes, the sooner you get the funds." Calvin said.

"I'll let you know." Jamaal told them as they both nodded and got up from the table.

"Alright Jamaal, we need to get going but it was good to see you." Calvin replied.

"It was good to see you too, thank you." Jamaal said.

"No problem, we look forward to hearing from you. I'm sure we don't have to tell you not to mention this conversation to a certain few family members do we?" Preston asked.

"Oh no, I won't tell any of them." Jamaal replied as Calvin and Preston nodded and walked out to the parking lot.

Later that evening when Jamaal and Ramon were back at their apartment, Jamaal looked at the cards Preston and Calvin gave to him and thought about their conversation as Ramon went on and on about his conversation with Myra. Jamaal really wanted to make the extra money to help cover expenses for school but he was worried because he knows there's a lot he doesn't know when it comes to the underlying reason that his mom and Tracy never wanted anything to do with their own family's church and why they made it clear that he didn't need to connect with them. Jamaal remembered hearing the fear behind his mom and Tracy's voice when they would talk about it which made him wonder what really happened. He still wanted to know what his mother meant when she told him there would be a breaking of day and a day of reckoning.

At the same time, what Calvin and Preston told him seemed easy enough and he figured he could quit once he made enough money to maintain. In that moment, Jamaal was pretty certain he was going to go against his mom's wishes and see what this was about not knowing what would be on the other side to all of this once he got there. But he felt desperate to do whatever was necessary to make the money he needed, even if it meant joining a church and submitting to a pastor that his own mother, aunt and cousin don't trust or want anything to do with.

"Jamaal, you good? You've been quiet ever since we got back today." Ramon said as they sat at the table eating snacks.

"Yeah, I'm okay. I was just thinking about some of the things my cousins were telling me after you went to see Myra." Jamaal replied.

"Right! I forgot to ask you how that went, I was so excited to have Myra say yes to me when I asked her out!" Ramon said as Jamaal laughed a little.

"It's alright, I get it. So Calvin and Preston offered me a really good opportunity to make some extra money with them and it could help with expenses." Jamaal said.

"Oh wow, they did? I mean, do you have to go to your uncle's church to do it?" Ramon asked as Jamaal nodded.

"Yeah, I would have to join but you know how we're struggling and I don't feel I have any other choice since my mom isn't in a position to help me. They told me you can do this too if you want." Jamaal said.

"But wouldn't I have to join your uncle's church?" Ramon asked.

"Well, yeah but it sounds like a lot of money can be made and after those cars I saw my cousins in; I'll do anything at this point." Jamaal said as Ramon nodded.

"Yeah, I'm in the same boat you're in with my mom too and our dads don't care about us so we have to look out for ourselves." Ramon told him.

"Exactly, so you in? You're going to do this with me?" Jamaal asked.

"What exactly are we doing?" Ramon asked.

"The church has merchandise they sell to clients and you make a good profit based on how much they buy. Seems pretty simple if you ask me." Jamaal said.

"Oh wow, that's it? Yeah, that is simple. I'm assuming we would have to keep this a secret from everyone right?" Ramon asked.

"You got it! The weekends that our families come, we can lay low until they go back to Miami. But if we're in, the first meeting for new people is Friday night at eight at this location." Jamaal said, showing Ramon the card.

"Do you know where this place is?" Ramon asked.

"No but if you're in, I can see if Preston or Calvin could pick us up." Jamaal replied.

"I would rather we drive in case we decided we don't want to stay." Ramon said.

"I feel you but how will we do that when neither of us have a car?" Jamaal asked.

"I know someone who will let us use their car for the night so don't worry. Just let me know when to be ready Friday and I'm in." Ramon said as he and Jamaal slapped hands.

"Are you ready to get this money?" Jamaal asked.

"Man, I've been ready! If this goes like you cousins say, we can leave that dead end job we're at in no time!" Ramon said excitedly.

"That's the plan man, that's the plan. Like my cousins said, we can't do what our moms say all the time. We're adults now, so we can make our own decisions." Jamaal replied.

"You're right about that. So let's do this!" Ramon said.

Jamaal and Ramon spent the rest of the week at work and after school talking about their plans for going to the secret meeting at Time of Day on Friday night. Preston and Calvin were excited when Jamaal text them to let them know he was in and Ramon was coming with him. Jamaal knew that he was doing what he felt that he had to do to make money but felt bad about going against what his mom wanted and he knew how upset she and his Aunt Tracy would be if they found out what he was doing. Thursday afternoon, Jamaal's uncle, Pastor Walter Day, II picked them up from work so they could talk about a few things before they came tomorrow night. Since the church had Bible Study on Thursday nights, Jamaal and Ramon agreed to come so they could meet the other members and so Jamaal could reconnect with his other relatives.

Jamaal hadn't seen Walter or any of his other relatives since he was a little boy so he wasn't sure how he would respond to him when they saw each other. But to Jamaal's surprise, Walter welcomed him with open arms which made him feel a lot better. As they rode to the church in Walter's black Suburban, Jamaal asked him if he knew why his mom and his Aunt Tracy chose to cut all ties with their own family and keep him, his siblings and his other cousins away from everyone. Walter took a deep breath and smiled a little as he tried to think of a response to give Jamaal. He didn't say much more than his mom and Tracy did when he tried asking them. He said they had a disagreement some years ago that Tracy and Jamaal's mother never forgave them for but no one would say what it was which made Jamaal even more curious about what really happened.

The next night as Jamaal and Ramon start getting dressed to go to Time of Day, they hear a knock at the door. Ramon went to answer assuming it was his friend who had agreed to let him and Jamaal hold their car for the night but it was Jamaal's cousin, Earnest. He quickly walked past Ramon and stood face to face with Jamaal who couldn't figure out why he appeared to be so upset.

"What's up, Earnest? You good? You seem on edge!" Jamaal said, glancing at Ramon as he closed the door.

"My girlfriend called me yesterday and told me saw you and Ramon get into a black Suburban outside the campus. I know for a fact that Uncle Walter has a truck like that, did he pick you two up?" Earnest asked.

"No Earnest, he didn't pick us up! Why would he?" Jamaal asked, trying to hide the fact that he was nervous.

"What about Calvin and Preston? I told them to stay away from both of you, have they been bothering you?" Earnest asked.

"We ran into Calvin and Preston at one of the parties over the weekend but it was nothing more than a hello and a goodbye! That's why I didn't tell you." Jamaal replied as Earnest looked over at Ramon who was leaning up against their desk.

"Jamaal, you better not be lying to me! So none of them have tried inviting you to Time of Day or ask you about joining Uncle Walter's church?" Earnest asked.

"Oh my God, Earnest! No, they haven't! Are we going to do this every day? The truck we got into was one of Ramon's friends taking us back to the dorm after work, that was it." Jamaal said as Earnest sighed and paused a moment before responding.

"You two are dressed up for a Friday night? Where are you off to?" Earnest asked.

"One of my friends is having a birthday party tonight and everyone is supposed to wear black and dress formally." Ramon replied.

"Earnest, I know my mom and Aunt Tracy told you to look out for us but you're taking your job way too seriously with all these questions!" Jamaal said.

"Trust me Jamaal, if you knew what I knew about our family you would understand why. If I wasn't here, Aunt Katrina and my mom would not have let you come to school here. You know that right?" Earnest asked.

"Yes Earnest, I know! I know all the rules and I know Mom and Aunt Tracy want me to stay away from our relatives and we're doing that. I just don't understand why no one will tell us what has made my mom Aunt Tracy stay away from our family all these years." Jamaal said as Earnest shook his head.

"I'll admit, I've been wanting to know about that too. They never want to go into it but something obviously went down because I can hear in my mom's voice every time she happens to bring them up." Earnest said.

"Yeah, my mom responds the same way. Listen Earnest, don't worry. We're doing what they told us to do, I promise." Jamaal replied as he and Earnest slapped hands and hugged each other.

"Alright, just be careful and don't hesitate to call me no matter what." Earnest told them.

"We will..."

"Okay, I better get back home. I'll see you guys on Monday." Earnest said as he slapped hands with Ramon and walked out of their dorm room. Ramon and Jamaal sighed in relief.

"Oh my God! That was close, you did good man." Ramon said as he checked to see what time it was.

"Dang, I can't believe his girl saw us leave with Uncle Walter today. Luckily he believed me when I told him it was one of your friends." Jamaal said.

"Yeah but we may have just done all of that for nothing." Ramon said as she sat on the side of his bed looking at his phone.

"What do you mean?" Jamaal asked.

"My friend is working later than he thought so he won't be home for about two or three hours. Text your cousins and tell them we can't come." Ramon said as Jamaal shook his head.

"I can't believe this. Alright, let me text them now." Jamaal replied as he quickly grabbed his phone.

As Jamaal got ready to text Preston and Calvin, there was another knock at their door. Jamaal sighed in frustration thinking it was Earnest coming back to hassle them again and he initially wasn't going to answer it until he realized he heard a female's voice outside the door. Jamaal looked at Ramon and signaled for him to see who it was. Ramon opened the door and they saw a tall, slender brown skinned woman with long braids who didn't appear to be much older than they were.

"Hi, I think you might have the wrong room. The next set of girls dorms are across the walk from here." Ramon said as Jamaal walked over to where he was standing.
"Oh no, I'm not looking for the female dorm. Are you Jamaal and Ramon?" she asked as they glanced at each other.
"I'm Jamaal and this is Ramon. I'm sorry, do we know you?" Jamaal asked, confused as she laughed.
"Hey Jamaal, I wasn't expecting you to recognize me either. I'm your cousin, Natalia. Walter is my father." Natalia said as they shook hands and hugged each other.
"Oh my God, you're my cousin too! Nice to meet you, finally! This is my best friend, Ramon." Jamaal said as Ramon shook her hand.
"Nice to meet you. So you both look nice, are you ready for tonight?" Natalia asked.

"Well yeah, we were just about to text Preston to tell him our ride fell through and we couldn't come." Jamaal said.

"Well, I guess Preston and Calvin must have had a feeling this might happen because they sent me to pick you two up since I was getting ready to leave campus and head out there." Natalia said as Jamaal and Ramon looked surprised.

"Oh wow, are you serious? We didn't even know you were coming but we're glad you're here!" Jamaal said as Natalia started laughing.

"Yeah, they had a feeling you were going to need a lift." Natalia told them.

"So you're a student here too? I don't think we've ever seen you." Ramon said.

"I doubt it, I'm in graduate school and this is my last semester so I'm excited!" Natalia replied.

"Wow, that is awesome! Congrats! What are you studying?" Ramon asked.

"Clinical Psychology, I want to be a counselor." Natalia told them.

"That's great Natalia, I'm happy for you." Jamaal said.

"Thank you, I appreciate it. You guys ready? Preston and Calvin told me to get you out of here without Earnest seeing us." Natalia said as Ramon locked their door and the three of them started down the hall.

"Yeah, we should be okay if Earnest isn't outside hiding in a bush or something. He came by earlier." Jamaal said as Natalia nodded.

"He came by your dorm earlier? What did he say?" she asked as they walked outside to her red Mercedes parked in front of the building.

"Man, this is nice! I hope to ride like this one day!" Ramon said as he and Jamaal slapped hands.

"Thank you and if you stick with us, you will one day!" Natalia said as Jamaal got in the front seat.

"You really think we will make that much money selling products?" Ramon asked.

"Most definitely! That's how it happened for me, Preston, Calvin and a lot of other people. You will see, just wait!" Natalia replied as she backed out of the parking lot and started driving down the street. "So Jamaal, tell me what Earnest said."

"Oh yeah, that. So he showed up to our dorm in a panic. His girlfriend saw us get into your dad's truck yesterday when he came to get us for Bible Study." Jamaal said as Natalia sighed and shook her head.

"That's not good. So he knows now?" Natalia asked.

"No, I told him that it was one of Ramon's friends who picked us up to throw him off. I honestly don't know if he fully believed me but he let it go and kept stressing about how we can't come to the church and to stay away from all of you." Jamaal said.

"Yeah, I figured that would happen and I'll let the guys know when we get there. But you agreed to come so that let's me know that you are realizing that you're your own man and you can make your own decisions. Right?" Natalia asked.

"Yeah, that's right. I mean, I don't want to worry my mom so I'm still trying to keep all of this a secret but working at this coffee shop is not cutting it for us anymore and our moms are working to take care of our other siblings so they can't really help us." Jamaal said.

"I get that, I do. Listen, we all felt bad when my dad told us about your accident and how you couldn't play ball after your injuries. We knew it was hard for you and my dad actually reached out to Aunt Katrina and Aunt Tracy saying he was willing to pay for you and Ramon's tuition but they refused to accept it." Natalia told them as Ramon and Jamaal glanced at each other in shock.

"Are you serious right now?" Jamaal asked.

"Oh wow, you guys didn't know huh?" Natalia asked.

"No, we didn't know that! We're out here struggling and my mom and our aunt ruined the only chance we had to make sure we had enough money for school?" Jamaal asked, disgusted.

"Man, so Ms. Trina and Ms. Tracy are really that mad huh?" Ramon asked.

"I guess they are but yeah, that was why we were going to find a way to tell you about the group so you could still make your money." Natalia replied.

"That makes sense but Uncle Walter could have given us the money when we got here couldn't he?" Jamaal asked.

"Yeah, he was going to do that. But he figured you would like it way more to make your own. You

will probably make three times as much, you'll see."
Natalia said, smiling as she continued driving.

"Yeah, I'm not used to handouts anyway."
Jamaal said.

"Me either, my mom always taught me to work
for what I want so this is good. Oh my God, where are
we going? Are we in the woods?" Ramon asked as he
looked over and realized they were riding into the
outskirts of the city.

"Yeah Natalia, we're not getting lost are we?"
Jamaal asked.

"Relax guys, we're not lost. We'll be there in
another ten minutes. The location is really big so my
dad purchased some property out here for the
location to keep it private." Natalia told them.

"Wow! This is far! So people come all the way
out here to buy products?" Jamaal asked.

"Yeah, it sort of works that way. Listen, I know
you probably have a million questions but that's what
tonight is for! You're going to get all of your questions
answered and you will have a good time too, that's
why you dressed up." Natalia said.

Jamaal and Ramon gasped when they finally
arrived at the location and saw how big it was with
lights everywhere and cars parked all over the place
including at the front with several guys dressed in all
black with white ties parking cars for different
customers. Natalia pulled up to the front of the valet
line and handed her keys to one of the staff as the
three of them got out of the car and started walking
towards the front door. Everything appeared to be

the way Natalia, Calvin and Preston were describing it. They saw different restaurants owned by the church along with a movie theatre, an arcade and a lounge.

As Natalia walked to them to the area where the new recruits were gathered, Jamaal couldn't help but wonder what it was his mom and aunt could have an issue with when it came to his uncle's church. But Jamaal would soon learn that things are not always what they appear to be, and everything that glitters isn't gold. After they arrived at the meeting area, Natalia walked out once she saw Walter, Calvin and Preston at the front of the room preparing to start their presentation. Jamaal was shocked when he saw how many other college students were in attendance. Ramon pointed something out to him that he didn't realize at first. All of the new recruits in the room were young men, there were no women in the meeting. As Jamaal thought about it more, he saw that the employees working in the stores were young men too who were all local college students. While it was odd, Jamaal decided no to make it an issue as the meeting started.

After Walter, Preston and Calvin finished their presentation, they walked them to another room that was adjacent to where they were sitting. When they walked inside, there were several rows of shelves that had uniforms in each of them. Each row was marked by size and not long after walking in, they were instructed to get three uniforms in their size and come back to the meeting area when they were done. Jamaal was excited to start after the presentation they gave and so was Ramon. As Jamaal and Ramon sat at their table talking and waiting for the meeting to resume, Jamaal felt his phone vibrate in his pocket and he decided to see who it was. It was a text message from Earnest wanting to see where he and Ramon were after noticing they weren't in their dorm when he came by again to talk to them. Jamaal shook his head and texted Earnest back telling him they were at their friend's party.

Earnest replied and asked for the address to the party they were at and that was when Jamaal glanced at Ramon who was drinking a soda and looking at messages on his phone. It was obvious that Earnest had only sent these messages to him and not Ramon. Jamaal placed his phone on the table in front of him and decided not to reply hoping Earnest would back off. Moments later, Earnest sent another text message and asked Jamaal if he and Ramon were at Time of Day. Jamaal panicked, wondering if Earnest had followed them or if he saw them leave with Natalia earlier. Jamaal quickly replied back and said that he didn't know what that was. When Earnest text again and asked if they were with Walter or any of their other cousins, Jamaal said they weren't and told him he would call him tomorrow since they were at the party. Earnest didn't say anything else after that and Jamaal took a deep breath.

Ramon nudged him and asked if he was okay when he saw his expression change and Jamaal shook his head and told them they had to go as he quickly grabbed his things and ran out of the room. Ramon was confused but quickly went after Jamaal to see what was wrong. Jamaal started down a hallway that didn't have a lot of people as Ramon trailed behind him calling for him and asking Jamaal to stop so they could talk. Jamaal and Ramon went out of a side door that brought them to another large building behind the one they were in. Jamaal finally stopped running to catch his breath as he dropped his things in front of him and took a drink from his water bottle.

"Jamaal, what's going on man? Why did you just run out like that? Did someone call you or something?" Ramon asked, confused.

"We need to go back to the dorm before we get caught. Where's Natalia?" Jamaal asked as he started looking around for her.

"Bro, what are you talking about? Get caught by who?" Ramon asked.

"Man, Earnest text a moment ago. He said he came back to the dorm to talk to us and saw we weren't there." Jamaal said as Ramon's expression changed.

"Why would he come back? We told him we were going to a party." Ramon said.

"My point exactly! I told him we were at the party and then he asked for the address. I tried to ignore him after that and I just told him we were partying and I would call him tomorrow." Jamaal said.

"So did he step off after that?" Ramon asked.

"No, he asked if we were at Time of Day! How would he know that if he didn't follow us out here? Or he must have seen us leave with Natalia!" Jamaal said in a panic as Ramon tried to calm him down.

"Hold on Jamaal, wait a minute! I get why you're freaking out but calm down and think! If Earnest knew we were here, don't you think your mom and your aunt would be blowing you up right now about it?" Ramon asked as Jamaal nodded.

"Yeah, that's true. I guess Earnest is just getting more and more suspicious but how long do you think we're going to be able to keep him off our backs before he figures out what's going on?" Jamaal asked as Ramon sighed and thought for a moment.

"Man, I'm not sure but I know I'm not going to let him, your mom, your aunt or anyone stop me from making this money! Now I know I'm not related to you and my mom was on your mom and aunt's side about me staying away from this place too but if I gotta be a member at your uncle's church to make this money then I'll do it! Did you see how much Preston said we would make in the first week?" Ramon asked, excitedly!

"Yeah man, it's going to be good for us!" Jamaal said as they sapped hands.

"That's right! So don't let Earnest work you up. We'll be good if we play it cool like we've been doing. He can only stay suspicious for so long." Ramon said as Jamaal nodded.

"That's true..."

"Alright then, you good now? Can we go back?" Ramon asked.

"Yeah let's go back in. I appreciate you." Jamaal said as they slapped hands again and headed back inside.

"Hey, there you guys are! We were walking all over the place looking for you. I guess I should have called you! Are you okay? Why did you run out?" Walter asked as he, Preston and Calvin approached them in the hall.

"I'm sorry Uncle Walter, I'm good now. Earnest was blowing me up and I got worried that he knew Ramon and I were out here." Jamaal said as Walter, Preston and Calvin glanced at each other.

"Did he say he knows you're here?" Calvin asked.

"No but I think he's suspicious. He kept asking questions and I panicked. I'm sorry." Jamaal said as Walter nodded and hugged him.

"You're okay Nephew, we got you. Listen don't worry about Earnest, just stay cool and you will be okay." Walter replied.

"See Jamaal, I told you so." Ramon said as Jamaal took a deep breath and nodded his head.

"I'm sorry for running out, I just panicked. I mean, my mom and Aunt Tracy would freak out if they knew I was here with you guys and so would Ramon's mom." Jamaal said.

"We understand but I promise you after tonight, you're really not going to care what your mom or anyone else thinks about your decision. Trust us." Walter said with a smirk as Jamaal and Ramon nodded in agreement.

"Are you guys ready to continue? We have a lot more to show you." Preston said.

"Yeah, let's do it!" Jamaal replied.

Jamaal and Ramon came home late that night not realizing that what they encountered was more than a meeting for new employees, it was an induction. Jamaal woke up the next morning and he didn't feel the same and he realized Ramon felt the same way. For the first time ever they both started their day praying and reading their Bible that was given to them at church Thursday night. While praying and reading the Bible wasn't wrong, it's their interpretation of belief when it came to God and the Bible that was different than before. By the time Jamaal left church on Sunday, a deep brainwashing had taken place that he couldn't explain and neither could Ramon. Jamaal was ready to embrace what he was feeling and continue the bond he was finally starting to build with his uncle, Walter and his other family. Ramon however wasn't as ready to commit. He wanted to do whatever it took to remain in the group to make money but he didn't realize joining the church would place this type of demand one one person's commitment.

Jamaal and Ramon returned back to their dorm around five late that afternoon after having dinner at Walter's house with the rest of his family. Ramon was planning to tell Jamaal how he was feeling about all this and his intentions of backing out of the group and going back to work at the cafe. After only a couple of days in, all of this was too much for Ramon and he couldn't help but think that Jamaal's mom and aunt may really have good reason to want Jamaal to stay away from them even though he didn't know the reasons why. As Jamaal and Ramon got off the elevator and walked to their front door, they saw Earnest's girlfriend, Dana standing outside of their door with tears coming down her face. Jamaal and Ramon knew something had to be wrong as they approached her and she asked if they could talk inside.

"Dana, what's going on? Is Earnest okay?" Jamaal asked in a concerned tone as the three of them sat down.

"Well, he'll be fine I guess but that's why I came to talk to you instead of him. He's really upset and I wanted him to heal and not risk running into your other cousins again so I came." Dana said as Ramon hander her tissue.

"I'm confused, what's going on? Is Earnest hurt or something?" Jamaal asked.

"Yeah, he got beat up pretty bad and he won't let me call the police and he won't even let me take him to the hospital. He said he can't or it will be worse next time." Dana replied as Jamaal reacted to what she said.

"What? Earnest was beat up? Where is he?" Jamaal asked standing up.

"He's at home but sit down, I can't take you to see him right now." Dana said.

"Why not? Does my mom and his mom know about this?" Jamaal asked.

"No, he didn't want to tell them yet and he's mad at you Jamaal. He kept saying this was your fault." Dana replied as Jamaal looked confused and glanced at Ramon who was shaking his head.

"He said this is my fault? How could something I knew nothing about before now be my fault? Does he know who hurt him?" Jamaal asked, sternly.

"Earnest couldn't see their faces, it was dark and they were wearing masks. But they told him to mind his business and keep his mouth shut so he figured it was probably some of your cousins sent to warn him by your uncle, Walter." Dana said.

"What? Okay, I know they don't get along but they wouldn't hurt Earnest like that. We're family!" Jamaal said.

"Jamaal, I don't usually try to get in your family business but this is my man we're talking about here! He's all banged up and he's too afraid to let anything be done about it. So I'm going to talk to you and I need you to tell me the truth." Dana said.

"What is it?" Jamaal asked.

"Have you been to your uncle's church or this secret group they have? Be honest!" Dana said.

"No, I haven't. No one has even asked me anything about the church or the group! They know my mom isn't down for it." Jamaal said as Dana sighed a moment before responding.

"What about that truck I saw you and Ramon get into on Thursday, that wasn't your uncle Walter?" Dana asked.

"Earnest asked me the same thing and just like I told him, no! It wasn't Walter, it was someone else that is friends with Ramon. We were just going out after work, that was it." Jamaal said.

"Are you sure Jamaal?" Dana asked.

"Yes Dana, I'm positive." Jamaal said as Dana nodded.

"Alright, I'll tell Earnest what you said and maybe when he's calmed down some he'll come to you himself. But I'll be honest with you Jamaal, he may not believe you when I tell him what you said to me. He really thinks Walter sent your cousins to rough him up so he wouldn't keep reminding you of what your mom and your aunt told you. He thinks you're already involved, he just doesn't have proof." Dana said.

"I understand he's upset Dana but I'm not involved in anything. I'm a student working to stay above water and that's it! So he can believe whatever he wants but that's real and he better not tell my mom or Aunt Tracy otherwise! Look, I want to come check on him but you said he's mad so have him call me when he's ready to talk to me." Jamaal said as Dana grabbed her things and headed for the door.

"Okay, I'll tell him. I'll see you guys later." Dana replied as she walked and closed the door behind her.

Jamaal and Ramon both sighed in relief after she walked out. Jamaal managed to keep his composure while talking to Dana but he knew she and Earnest's suspicions were right. Jamaal didn't know his cousins were going to go after him like that but he wasn't surprised. They all seem bothered Friday night when he explained why he ran out of the meeting the way he did. But he didn't know they would do anything like this to their own family.

Jamaal walked over to his bed and turned his back to Ramon as he sent a text message on his phone. Moments later, he hears noise and he quickly turns around to see what was going on. Ramon had pulled out his suitcases onto his bed and began packing his clothes as if he was getting ready to leave and Jamaal became confused as he walked over to his side of the room to see what was wrong.

"Ramon, where are you going? Why are you packing your clothes?" Jamaal asked.

"Look man, this is just getting too weird for me and I'm getting out of here! I won't tell anyone that you joined your uncle's church or what we did Friday night but I'm going home. I'll just live with my mom, help her and go to school there like she wanted in the first place!" Ramon said in a panic as he continued to pack his clothes.

"Ramon, wait a minute! Talk to me first!" Jamaal said as Ramon stopped packing, took a deep breath and sat in a chair next to his bed.

"Listen, I know I was down for all of this at first because I wanted money but I'd rather stay broke if this is what I have to deal with!" Ramon said.

"What are you talking about? You're worried about Earnest? We don't even know for sure it was anyone in my family, it could have been a random robbery or something!" Jamaal said defensively.

"Do you really believe his attack was random?" Ramon asked as Jamaal sighed and paused for a moment before responding.

"I guess I don't know for sure but my people wouldn't do that!" Jamaal replied.

"Jamaal, how do you really know that? You're just really getting to know this side to your family so you don't know what they're capable of or what steps they will take to make sure they don't get busted by people like your mom and your aunt!" Ramon said.

"I get that Ramon but I don't want you to panic and go home just because of what happened. Earnest will be fine." Jamaal said.

"It's not just Earnest I'm worried about. If anything, Earnest getting attacked like this only makes me want out of this mess even more! Bro, look at me! It hasn't even been a week and I don't feel the same. I talk differently, my mind is thinking about stuff I never thought about before or believed in and I don't like it!" Ramon said in a stern tone.

"Ramon, that is all a part of the process of growing closer to God!" Jamaal replied as Ramon laughed sarcastically.

"Oh my God! Your uncle got you brainwashed already too! Are you listening to yourself? Bro we didn't come into this to be some holy rollers! We wanted to make money and that was it and now look at us! We haven't made anything yet but we're walking around here like some freaking altar boys who want to go to seminary or some mess? C'mon Jamaal, you know that's weird!" Ramon said as Jamaal shook his head.

"Ramon, you're my boy and I love you but I can't let you do this." Jamaal said.

"Let me do what, Jamaal?" Ramon asked.

"Talk about my pastor like this! In the short time we've known him, he's been the father to us we never had!" Jamaal said as Ramon became upset.

"Oh you're really losing it! Pastor Walter is not my daddy and I'm not letting him be anything to me! Are you serious?" Ramon asked, disgusted by Jamaal's reaction and sudden change of behavior.

"Yes, I'm serious! Listen Ramon, you don't need to leave. I mean, I don't want to scare you but I'm more worried about what could happen if you decide to go." Jamaal said.

"Nothing would happen because I haven't taken anything from your uncle! All I have are these lame uniforms which I'll give back with no problem! So don't try to make me think I have something tying me to them!" Ramon said.

"Are you going to give back the money too? I don't strike my uncle as a man who lets dues go unpaid." Jamaal said as Ramon's expression changed.

"What money? Pastor Walter didn't give me any money!" Ramon said as Jamaal shook his head.

"You must have missed Preston's text this morning." Jamaal said as Ramon started looking through his phone.

"I don't see any messages from Preston, what are you talking about? What money?" Ramon asked.

"The direct deposit we set up wasn't just for payments after working. We got a signing bonus too. Check your account." Jamaal replied.

"A signing bonus? No one said anything about that!" Ramon said.

"It wasn't said out loud because everyone was going to get it, just the select ones who would eventually elevate to the elite roles. Check your account, the money should be there now." Jamaal said as Ramon shook his head in disbelief and pulled up his banking app on his phone.

"Oh my God!" he said.

"You see it?" Jamaal asked.

"What the heck is this? Ten thousand dollars, are you kidding me? You got it too?" Ramon asked.

"Yes, I have it. I thought you were paying attention so I didn't mention it. But yeah, we're in there man. We never have to work that dead end job on campus again!" Jamaal said.

"No way! I'm not taking this money! I'm going to give all of this back and I'm going back to Miami. Like I said, I won't tell anyone anything but I can't do this Jamaal and you need to leave with me!" Ramon said.

"Bro, I'm not leaving and if you don't want to be in then that's you. But don't go back home and get my mom and my aunt Tracy all suspicious. They're already going to freak out when they find out about Earnest, if they haven't found out already. They haven't texted me yet." Jamaal said as he looked at his phone.

"I don't really care if they get suspicious at this point because honestly Jamaal, I'm really starting to wonder if your mom and Ms. Tracy had good reason to tell us to stay away from your uncle's church. This stuff is crazy and none of it is worth the money. I just can't do it and you need to run while you have the chance!" Ramon said.

"Run from what? Listen Ramon, you do whatever you want to do but I'm not leaving my pastor for anyone! He's family!" Jamaal replied.

"I really can't believe what I'm hearing right now. Who are you and what have you done with my best friend?" Ramon asked as Jamaal shook his head.

"Stop playing around Ramon, this is me!" Jamaal said.

"No it's not and that's what I'm saying! We weren't talking like this before last night and now we're holier than thou? I'm not going to keep going back and forth with you about this, okay? I'm going to give this money and these uniforms back to Pastor Walter and I'm going home! I won't talk and everyone can think whatever they want but I'm not sticking around for this!" Ramon told him.

By the next morning, Ramon was more eager than ever to leave and go back. He couldn't figure it all out right then but after the experience he had Friday night at the gathering, he knew something wasn't right and while Jamaal didn't want to believe it; he knew there had to be a reason that Jamaal's mother and aunt wanted them to stay away from Walter's church. Ramon didn't want to see Walter or anyone from the church so he left his uniforms with Jamaal to give back to him when he got to church and he wired the money that Walter gave him back so he wouldn't owe anything or feel tied to them. Ramon packed his bags and waited outside to be picked up and taken to the airport so he could catch his flight back to Miami.

After Ramon left, Jamaal started thinking about Earnest and he really wanted to check on him before he went to church even though his girlfriend said he didn't want to see him. Jamaal took a deep breath and gathered his things and he caught the bus to Earnest's off campus apartment which wasn't far where he stayed. As Jamaal arrived at the complex, he received a text message from Preston who asked if he still needed a ride to church. Jamaal knew he probably wouldn't get back to his dorm before he arrived so he replied to Preston and gave him a location near the apartment complex to pick him up from. Preston agreed and said he would meet him there in an hour. Jamaal walked into the complex and headed to Earnest's building.

As he reached the top of the stairs where his apartment was, he saw Earnest's girlfriend getting ready to walk inside and called out to her as she finished her phone call. Jamaal walked up and begged her to ask Earnest to let him come in so they could talk. Jamaal stood at the door waiting as she went inside to let Earnest know that he was waiting to talk to him. Moments later, she came back to the door and nodded as she invited Jamaal inside. Earnest was sitting on the sofa in the living room watching television with bandages on his head and a cast on his right arm.

"Hey Earnest, thanks for letting me see you." Jamaal said as he pulled up a chair and sat across from him.

"I only let you in here because I'm hoping that after what happened to me, you're finally ready to talk and tell me the truth!" Earnest said in a stern tone as he turned off the television.

"Tell you the truth?" Jamaal asked.

"Yes Jamaal, tell me the truth! Where's Ramon?" Earnest asked.

"He's gone..."

"What do you mean he's gone?" Earnest asked in shock.

"He packed up his stuff and he left this morning to go back to Miami." Jamaal said.

"Really? Why did he leave all of a sudden? He was just as determined as you were to go to school here." Earnest said.

"Yeah, I know but he wanted to go back home. I guess he got homesick." Jamaal said.

"Yeah, I bet he would tell a different story if I were to talk to him and if you want to tell me the truth then you can leave." Earnest said in a stern tone.

"I don't know what you're talking about but if you want me to go then I'll go. I just wanted to check on you and see if you were okay." Jamaal said as he stood and gathered his things.

"Wow!" Earnest said as Jamaal became confused.

"What?" Jamaal asked.

"You see me here like this and you're really going to leave and pretend like you don't know how this happened?" Earnest asked.

"I don't know how it happened, Earnest! You won't tell me anything!" Jamaal said, sternly.

"Oh alright, let me help you out since you want to play dumb! Uncle Walter sent Preston, Calvin and two of our other cousins to beat me up because they felt like I was getting in the way of their plan!" Earnest said as Jamaal's expression changed and he sat back in the chair.

"So you saw their faces?" Jamaal asked.

"No, they were dressed in black wearing masks but they're our cousins and I know their voices!" Earnest said.

"You're assuming it was them when you don't know that for sure! What would make you think our own cousins would hurt you like this? I mean, you're wearing a cast right now! Are you able to play ball?" Jamaal asked.

"They messed my arm pretty bad and the doctor said I can come out of the cast in another three weeks but I'll never have full use of this arm again thanks to them!" Earnest said as tears fell down his face.

"Earnest, I'm sorry this happened to you and I want to be there for you but you're accusing our uncle and our cousins of hurting you. If they really did this to you, then why not tell the police?" Jamaal asked.

"Man are you serious? This, these injuries were just a warning! Uncle Walter will have me killed if I talk! Why do you think my mom and your mom have been silent for so long? Why do you think they told us to stay away from him and the church?" Earnest asked as Jamaal shook his head.

"Earnest, I'm sorry this happened to you but you still haven't explained how you know it was our cousins. You said they were wearing masks and voices can sound like anyone!" Jamaal replied.

"It's what they said to me that let me know it was them, Jamaal!" Earnest said.

"What did they say?" Jamaal asked.

"They told me I needed to keep my mouth shut and stay out of your ear! They said I'm getting in the way and if I get in the way again, I won't live to say another word about them to anyone! That's how I know!" Earnest said, enraged as his girlfriend brought him something to drink along with his dose of pain medication.

"That's what they said?" Jamaal asked, surprised.

"Yes, that is what they said verbatim! So no, I'm not in a rush to tell the cops anything because I'll be dead before an arrest is ever made! Then Uncle Walter has a bunch of lawyers including two of his daughters who will get him off if it ever came to that! With all the illegal mess he's in, he has to have his dream team of attorneys to avoid jail time! But it is all at a cost! Two souls were sacrificed for them to have everything you see!" Earnest said as Jamaal became confused again.

"What are you talking about, Earnest?" Jamaal asked.

"Look, you will find that out soon enough. Since you don't want to come clean, let me call you out. I know you lied about your involvement with Uncle Walter! You and Ramon were acting suspicious and I couldn't put my finger on it at first. I didn't want to believe you would be with Uncle Walter after the promises you made to your mom and my mom to stay away but I just wasn't sure after that truck my girl saw you get in that day. So I went to your old job." Earnest said.

"Why?" Jamaal asked.

"I wanted to do my own investigation! When the manager told me you two showed up and quit out of the blue, I knew something was up! I knew Uncle Walter found a way to get you and Ramon into their cult by offering you money and the chance to make extra money to stay in school. That's how gets all his new recruits! So you still want to lie to me?" Earnest asked as Jamaal sighed and paused a moment.

"Okay fine, you're right. Preston and Calvin approached us at the party we had before school started back. They told us about the business and how much money we could. Ramon and I weren't going to do it at first but we couldn't keep going at the rate we were at. That part-time job wasn't helping and we lost our chance for a full ride scholarship like yours because of our accident. So we got desperate and we joined! Are you happy now?" Jamaal asked.

"Wait a minute! So Earnest was right? You and Ramon joining this cult is the reason he's sitting here in cast and won't be able to play ball again?" Dana asked.

"I didn't mean for this to happen, I'm sorry. We just wanted to make more money!" Jamaal said as Dana shook her head and walked into the kitchen.

"Jamaal, you have always been stubborn and you've never been one to listen to people when you think you know something. Do you know what you and Ramon signed up for? I know you went to that party Friday and you saw all those stores with college students in them but that is a cover up! They make a the bulk of their money through pornography and the strip club they have." Earnest said.

"What? They didn't show us anything like that while we were there Earnest and we took a tour!" Jamaal said.

"They only showed you what they wanted you to see, Jamaal. The buildings where the strip club and where they do their videos for porn sites was behind the main building towards the back of the property. It's a possibility you saw it but paid it no attention because the building is black." Earnest said as Jamaal thought for a moment.

"Wait a minute, we actually saw those buildings when Ramon and I happened to walk outback during the meeting. That's what that was?" Jamaal asked.

"Yes, that's what that was. Once you and Ramon would have made it through your six month probation period, they would have told you about that next and that would have blown your mind." Earnest told him.

"Why is that?" Jamaal asked.

"I'm sure a few girls you know from school make their money dancing and doing videos. The money is decent but I can assure you it's not worth what it will ultimately cost you in the end." Earnest said.

"I don't know if I believe you at this point Earnest. I mean Uncle Walter is a good pastor and he would never do anything like this!" Jamaal replied as Earnest laughed sarcastically.

"Wow! He got you and Ramon calling him Pastor now? Oh wait, that's right! You said Ramon went home right?" Earnest aked.

"Yeah, he went home because he didn't like the way he felt after we came home Friday night. He didn't feel like himself and he felt something was wrong. He thought there was some truth to what my mom and Aunt Tracy told us so he gave the money back, left the uniforms and he's on a plane back to Miami now." Jamaal said as Earnest nodded.

"Wow! Well at least your best friend came to his senses and didn't die in this mess like mine did." Earnest replied as Jamaal's expression changed.

"What are you talking about?" Jamaal asked.

"The reason I know about Uncle Walter's dealings the way I do is because I thought I was going to sneak behind my mom and Aunt Katrina's back too and join. I had my best friend with me at the time but things took a turn. My friend died and they ruled a suicide but I think they killed him." Earnest said.

"Why would they want to do that?" Jamaal asked.

"When we hit our six months and went to the strip club, my friend saw one of his sisters dancing on the pole and he lost it! He charged at Uncle Walter, knocked him to the floor and a bunch of our cousins got him before he could actually hit him. Next thing I know, I get a call the next day about him being found in his dorm dead from some apparent overdose but I never agreed with that. I tried talking to the cops and asked them to investigate and I was going to expose Uncle Walter back then but he apparently has some rank there too because as soon as I said Walter Day, they had me leave." Earnest replied.

"I'm sorry Earnest, you never told me you lost a friend to all of this. That's hard." Jamaal said.

"Well, I hope Ramon doesn't plan to talk when he gets back or he will likely be next." Earnest said.

"He said he wasn't going to say anything but I know Mom and Aunt Tracy will be suspicious about him coming home so sudden and alone." Jamaal said.

"Yeah, they are and they may even show up here to finally take a stand. It would be nice to see because they have suffered the most from all of this!" Earnest said.

"Earnest, I have to get going. Preston and Calvin are on their way to a nearby store to pick me up for church. I'll call you later." Jamaal replied as he grabbed his things and started to open the door.

"Hold on a minute Jamaal, let me tell you this before you walk out of here! If you don't stop trying to cover Uncle Walter and see this mess for what it really is, you will be ruined in more ways than one! My mom and Aunt Katrina had a feeling you would get tempted to check things out so they begged me to talk to you, Ramon too but Ramon isn't blood. Our moms didn't want the cycle to repeat itself so she asked me to do everything in my power to keep you from getting curious because they knew the temptation would come and I tried my best. I told you over and over again to stay away and you kept saying you were going to stay away. You lied to me, you lied to your mother thinking you were grown and now look at what has happened. You've tied my hands and I really can't help you at this point." Earnest said.

"You're acting like I'm in danger or something, Earnest. Uncle Walter is my pastor and he wouldn't hurt anyone or me!" Jamaal replied defensively.

"Wow Jamaal, he really has you brainwashed! Trust me, Walter is not covering you the way you think he is and I don't know what made Ramon leave the way he did but he couldn't have made a better decision!" Earnest said.

"Well, that's how you feel but I'm sticking by my pastor so if you guys can't understand that, I'll accept it." Jamaal said.

Jamaal left Earnest's apartment moments after that and he rushed to meet Preston and Calvin who were minutes away from the location he agreed to meet them at. To avoid more problems, Jamaal wasn't planning to tell them about his conversation with Earnest. As much as he wanted to believe his pastor, he couldn't help but wonder if there was truth to what Earnest was telling him. Earnest was right about the fact that it was Preston, Calvin and two of their other cousins who attacked him and he was right about their reasons for attacking him. What Jamaal couldn't see was that Walter had a plan for him from day one to turn him against what his mother and aunt had been telling him about their church by inducting him into their cult and shifting his mind to a place where no matter what's said, he won't believe it. Walter's biggest fear was Jamaal one day coming into knowledge of the real reasons behind why his mother and aunt left the church without ever returning.

Walter was afraid of what would be revealed if Jamaal ever came into the knowledge of the truth so he had to do whatever it took to make sure that never happened. Jamaal has yet to see the trap he's walked into. It looks like he found a safe place to be accepted and for the first time ever, have the love of a father through Walter. But it's unfortunate that everything he feels is a set up for destruction if the covers aren't pulled back in time.

When Jamaal arrived at church, he gave Ramon's uniforms to Preston and Calvin to give back to Walter as they walked inside the main sanctuary. When service was over, Jamaal went to Walter's office to talk to him. He walks into the office and sees Walter, Preston and Calvin sitting at a table talking while they wait for him to arrive. Jamaal had a pretty good idea of what this conversation was going to be about and he was worried about Walter's reaction to Ramon leaving.

"Hey Jamaal, are you okay?" Walter asked as he sat down.

"I'm a little nervous I guess. I know you weren't expecting Ramon to leave like he did." Jamaal said as Walter nodded a little.

"Well no, I wasn't but that's not your fault. I'm sure you tried talking some sense into him before he left." Walter replied.

"Yes sir, I did. I tried but he left anyway. Did he refund you the money like he said?" Jamaal asked.

"Yeah, I saw that and that's fine. My biggest concern is what he will say once he's back home and your mom and Tracy start asking questions." Walter said.

"I asked Ramon about that before he left and he said he won't say anything." Jamaal said as Walter glanced at Preston and Calvin who were sitting on each side of Jamaal.

"We don't know Ramon the way you do so based on what you know, do you believe him? You think he will keep quiet about what he saw Friday night?" Walter asked.

"Yes sir, I think he will. He never said he wanted to expose anything. He just couldn't handle all of this like he thought." Jamaal replied.

"Well I hope you're right about that Jamaal. I would hate to confront Ramon because he can't keep his mouth shut. If he thinks being in Miami would keep that from happening, he has another thing coming if he says anything. Have you talked to your mom or Tracy?" Walter asked.

"No sir, they haven't called me yet. I'm assuming Ramon hasn't made it back yet but I'm sure they will be calling once he gets back though." Jamaal said.

"Have you checked on Earnest?" Walter asked.

"Yes sir, I did this morning. He didn't want to see me at first but I just wanted to make sure he was okay." Jamaal replied.

"Oh, so that's why we picked you up from the store instead of your dorm?" Calvin asked.

"Yeah, I knew I wouldn't make it back on the bus in time so I met you there instead." Jamaal said as Calvin nodded.

"So how is Earnest doing?" Walter asked.

"He's okay I guess. He said he won't be able to play basketball anymore which is crazy because he's here on a full ride scholarship. I don't know what he will do if he can't play." Jamaal said in a concerned tone.

"That's too bad but hopefully something works out for him soon. What did he say to you when you went there?" Walter asked.

"He didn't say a lot. He basically just told me what his doctors said about his injuries and he was trying to figure out what he would do next." Jamaal said, trying to avoid telling them what Earnest actually told them.

"Does he know who hurt him?" Preston asked.

"I asked him if he knew and he said he didn't know because the guys had on black and they were wearing masks. Plus it happened at night." Jamaal told him.

"Did he say anything else?" Walter asked.

"No, that was it. I didn't stay long because he was still resting when I went by his apartment." Jamaal told them.

"Jamaal, you know how much I love you right?" Walter asked.

"Yes, of course! I love you too!" Jamaal replied.

"That's good and I believe you. I know your father wasn't there and had your mom allowed me, I could have been there for you much sooner than now but we're connected now and that is what matters." Walter said.

"Yes sir..."

"Not to scare you Jamaal but I need to know that you're all in with me no matter what happens next." Walter said.

"Of course, I'm all in but what do you mean? Is something wrong?" Jamaal asked, confused.

"It's not that there's anything wrong, but people are always trying to come against us by saying things to ruin what took me and my parents years to build. There's nothing we won't do to protect our brand and as long as you have that same mind, there's nothing we won't do to make sure you're protected as well. Do you understand what I'm saying?" Walter asked.

"Yes Uncle Walter, of course! I understand and I have your back just like you have mine!" Jamaal replied as Walter, Preston and Calvin nodded.

"I knew I could count on you! I love you Jamaal." Walter said as he and Jamaal hugged each other.

"I love you too." Jamaal replied.

"Alright, I need to do some other things before I go home. Did you need anything else from me? Do you have enough money?" Walter asked.

"Oh yeah, I'm good. Thank you." Jamaal said.

"Great! Boys, take Jamaal back to his dorm and call me later on." Walter said as he got ready to leave his office for another meeting.

"Yes sir, let's go Jamaal." Preston replied as they grabbed their things and walked out behind Walter.

Jamaal didn't have classes Monday so he was able to sleep in after a long day yesterday. Around noon, he heard his phone vibrate multiple times as he laid in his bed and he woke up to see who was trying to reach out to him. Jamaal sees several messages from his mom saying they needed to talk and he figured Ramon must have made it back home and they were suspicious now. Jamaal was going to ignore the messages until he looked at the last message sent five minutes ago from his mom saying that she and his aunt, Tracy were in Gainesville and had just checked into the hotel. Katrina sent the address of the hotel to Jamaal and told him he needed to come and meet with her and Tracy as soon as possible or they would come visit him at his dorm. waiting to talk to him when he woke up. Jamaal knew if he didn't go meet them, they would show up at his dorm so he reluctantly replied to his mom's text and told her he would be there in thirty minutes.

As Jamaal got ready to leave, he looked out his window and saw Walter arrive in the parking lot with Preston, Calvin and three of his other cousins. He didn't know why they were coming to see him but he didn't want to explain where he was going or run the risk of being followed. Jamaal quickly grabbed his things and left his room and took the stairs instead of the main elevator hoping he could exit on the opposite of the dorm without seeing them. Moments after he got on the bus, he received a text message from Calvin asking where he was after explaining they were at his door.

Jamaal sighed as he thought about how he would respond to their message without raising suspicion. He eventually responded and told them he was meeting up with some friends to study for a big test he had next week. Calvin replied and said that was okay and asked him to call Walter when he was back so they could discuss a few things about their next meeting and another new recruit party they were planning to host again this Friday night. What Walter wasn't aware of was that Katrina and Tracy's arrival was by design and the reputation of his ministry would be challenged in a way that reveals what the four walls has spent years trying to hide.

Jamaal arrived at the hotel and immediately went to Katrina and Tracy's room to talk to them. When Katrina let Jamaal into the room, he was expecting to see Ramon and was surprised that he wasn't with them. Jamaal hugged his mom and Tracy before the three of them sat at the table near the window inside the room. Jamaal was nervous because he knew he left his mom and his aunt down by not following their instructions. But Jamaal was hoping he could convince his mom and aunt that he made the best decision by joining Walter's church, not knowing that he was about to be given the answers he sought for years ago from his mother.

"You're looking for Ramon?" Katrina asked.

"Yeah, I thought he would be with you even though he just left." Jamaal said.

"He was going to come with us but we didn't want to have to bring your brothers with us too so we left Ramon in Miami to watch them. Plus he needed to spend some time with his mom." Katrina said.

"I understand. So did he tell you why he came back?" Jamaal asked.

"Yeah, we pulled it out of him. He didn't want to talk at first and literally broke down when we asked him. He didn't want anyone else to get hurt after finding out what happened to Earnest." Tracy said.

"How did you get him to talk?" Jamaal asked.

"We promised him that he would be safe and that our parents, Walter and the rest of our brothers would all be held accountable once and for all. Once that happens, they're not going to have time to hurt anyone because they will be exposed and they will be the ones facing charges!" Katrina said as Jamaal looked confused.

"I don't understand." Jamaal replied.

"We're going to help you understand in just a moment. But after what happened to your cousin, do you see now why Tracy and I told you to stay away from your uncle's church?" Katrina asked.

"Mama, I don't think it was them. I mean, Earnest is not even sure. He said he couldn't see their faces." Jamaal said as defensively.

"Wow! Looks like our brother really got you brainwashed. If you knew what we knew, you wouldn't be defending him right now! He sent Calvin, Preston and probably two of Preston's other brothers to hurt Earnest! It doesn't matter if he didn't see their faces! He heard their voice and he heard what they said!" Katrina said, sternly.

"But why hurt him? He didn't do anything to them and plus we're family!" Jamaal said.

"You're about to find out that our relation to each other doesn't mean anything to your grandparents and your uncles! Now we're mad at you for not listening to us but we understand at the same time." Katrina said.

"You do?" Jamaal asked, surprised.

"Yes, we do. You should have listened to us Jamaal but I know you and Ramon were trying to stay afloat with money since you weren't able to play basketball. I knew Walter would find a way to present the idea of making more money to you which was why I wanted you to just stay in Miami to attend college so you could live at home. But you still wanted to go away to school like you planned to do with Ramon so we talked to Earnest." Katrina said.

"I get it. That was why he was always telling us to stay away and he was always checking on us. Right?" Jamaal asked.

"Yes Jamaal, that's right! When Ramon told us everything that happened with the two of you joining the church and working at their secret business, Earnest's attack made more sense. They felt like he was getting in the way of what they wanted to do with you and Ramon but especially you. So they hurt Earnest to shut him up!" Katrina said.

"Jamaal, Walter had your cousins hurt Earnest whether you choose to believe us or not. I know he's your pastor and whatever but he can't be trusted and you're about to see why." Tracy said as Jamaal shook his head.

"But Uncle Walter has been looking out for me. He's been acting like the dad I never had. I mean, I still to this day don't much about my dad and I appreciate everything you've done for me Mama but I didn't realize how much I needed my father until I connected with Uncle Walter. I just don't know if I'm ready to give that up." Jamaal said as Katrina and Tracy glanced at each other.

"Jamaal, I know your father wasn't there and I'm sorry for not telling you more about him. We can have that conversation when this is over but there wasn't much to tell. He led me on, had sex with me and jumped ship when he found out I was pregnant with you. He wanted nothing to do with us! Baby, I understand how you feel about Walter but none of this is what you think it is." Katrina said as she tried to fight back tears.

"What do you mean Mama? Uncle Walter doesn't love me?" Jamaal asked as Katrina sighed and walked over to sit in front of him.

"Jamaal, I'm not saying Walter hates you but what he calls love isn't real love. Walter has wanted nothing more than to help my parents get back at Tracy and I for leaving our family's church the way we did. I know he did because he tried it with Earnest but it didn't work and I figured it wouldn't happen if Earnest looked out for you." Katrina said.

"Mama, I'm sorry for not listening to you and Aunt Tracy. Had I known it would get Earnest beat up, I wouldn't have let Preston and Calvin talk me or Ramon into anything." Jamaal said.

"Good, so you believe us now?" Tracy asked as Jamaal sighed and nodded his head.

"I mean, I wanted to think it wasn't everything you said but I know you wouldn't lie to me so if this is the truth then I'll go with it. But Mama, you never told me what happened to make you and Aunt Tracy leave. I mean, can you tell me now?" Jamaal asked as Katrina glanced back at Tracy who was sitting near the.

"Go ahead and tell him Katrina, he needs to
know everything and he needs to know exactly why
our family has been up to no good all these years! So
tell him!" Tracy replied in a stern tone.

"Okay Jamaal, I'm going to tell you what you've
been asking me for years. Tracy and I were the
youngest of our siblings and we were the only girls so
we were always getting into something." Katrina said.

"That's pretty normal right?" Jamaal asked.

"Yeah, it was normal until we ended up in a
situation we couldn't talk our way out of. There was
this big conference our dad (*your grandfather*) had to
preach at one summer when Tracy and I were in high
school. It was packed with churches from everywhere
and of course there were a lot of young people there
our age and a little older." Katrina told him.

"What happened?" Jamaal asked.

"One night during the conference, a bunch of
us decided to ditch the youth session they were
having and go to a party. One of the other teens there
had an older cousin who lived in the area we were in
and he invited us to a party that wasn't far from the
conference center. So we went assuming we could
come back before our parents realized where we
were." Katrina said.

"Were Uncle Walter, Uncle Cal and Uncle
Richard with you?" Jamaal asked.

"Yeah, they were with us but with them being
older than us, they were paying more attention to
their friends and the girls their age. We were dancing
and having a good time and that was when two of our
overseer's sons approached us and asked if we

wanted to go down the hall. We said yes and we went with them." Katrina said.

"Where did they take you?" Jamaal asked.

"They took us to an empty room that was upstairs. The boys were eighteen and nineteen at the time. I was fifteen and Tracy sixteen but we thought it was cool to be with older boys but then things started moving too fast and we told them to stop and they got mad. They thought we were being a tease and they slapped us to the bed when we tried to run out the room screaming for our brothers and they got on top of us and raped us." Katrina said as tears fell down her and Tracy's faces.

"Oh my God! Mama, Aunt Tracy I didn't know! I am so sorry that happened to you." Jamaal said, sadly as he went to hug his mom and Tracy.

"Thank you baby, we appreciate that." Katrina said as Jamaal sat back down.

"So did my uncles hear you screaming?" Jamaal asked.

"No, they couldn't hear us because the music was too loud. I don't even think they knew we were upstairs with those boys because we didn't tell them where we were going." Katrina replied.

"So these guys raped you at the party. Did you tell anyone?" Jamaal asked.

"Not right away but the next day we did. When Tracy and I finally came out of the room, our brothers were calling for us because we needed to get back to the conference center because the services for the night were about to end. I remember our brothers looking at us and they were asking if we were okay and we said yeah and just took off running with the rest of them to get back so we wouldn't get caught." Katrina said.

"Okay, so when did you tell our family what happened to you? I mean I know my grandpa and my uncles were ready to kill those guys when you told them what they did right?" Jamaal asked, glancing at Tracy who gave a smirk.

"Tracy and I got up the next morning and told our parents where we were and they were getting upset at first and they called our brothers in the room before we could explain what happened. So now our brothers are mad because we told our parents what we did. But we got them to calm down and when they did we told them what the boys did. We told them and at first they were freaking out about it, ready to find out who did it so they could hurt them. But that all changed when I told them the name of the guys." Katrina said as Jamaal's expression changed.

"What changed? No one did anything once you told them who it was?" Jamaal asked.

"Yeah, pretty much. Our parents and our three older brothers who promised to protect us did nothing! Those boys father was the overseer and was the man to get your foot in the door when you wanted to start your church and make lots of money and my parents weren't going to let what happened mess that up for them." Katrina said.

"I really can't believe what I'm hearing right now! So they made you keep quiet about what they did to you?" Jamaal asked, disgusted.

"Yeah, they did. They even tried blaming us by saying that had we stayed at church like we were supposed to, we would not have been at a party getting raped. Our brothers at the time were in their early twenties at the time and they could have helped us when our parents refused but they didn't, they took our parents' side because all of them wanted to be in ministry too and our dad threatened to cut them off if they said anything about what happened. He told us to let it go and that was the last time it ever came up." Katrina said as Jamaal handed his mom tissue.

"Mama, I had no idea! So did you guys leave the church right then?" Jamaal asked.

"We wanted to but we were too young. We couldn't move out, we were in school with no jobs. But when Tracy turned nineteen and when I turned eighteen, we left. We packed up our stuff and moved to Miami with nothing but our bags and fifty dollars to our name. We were sleeping wherever we could for a couple of weeks and that was when we met Ramon's mother, Shea. She was about four years older than us at the time she was a dancer at a club and she had her own place. She didn't know us but she took us in, got us jobs at the club and that's what we were doing. We didn't quit dancing until after we all had our kids and started getting a little older. One of the girls who worked with us ended up losing custody of her children when someone reported her and we didn't want that to happen so we stopped and got regular jobs. Things were hard but we were determined to see our kids do better than us and we were going to do it with the church, without our family and without God." Katrina said as Jamaal nodded.

"Mama, can I ask you something else?" Jamaal asked.
"Yes..."
"What happened to the guys that raped you and Aunt Tracy? Are they still around? Is their father still the overseer?" Jamaal asked.
"He remained the overseer up until my father was ordained as an Apostle by that overseer and when Walter started the church, he was put into our dad's network. But everything you saw in that church was paid for at our expense!" Katrina said as Jamaal paused a moment to think about what his mom said.
"Are you saying that the overseer paid them to keep quiet about what his sons did to you and Aunt Tracy that night?" Jamaal asked.
"Yes, you got it! About six months after our assault, I guess my dad started feeling bad for not doing anything so he confronted the overseer about what happened and instead of having his sons arrested, he wrote a check and agreed to ordain my dad as an Apostle and our dad accepted it. The money paid for every last thing you saw in the church, it funds that illegal nonsense they have disguised as a store!" Katrina said.

"There's no telling how many other young women may have been taken advantage of in that place and nothing was done and they were probably paid to keep quiet. I know we should have spoken up a long time ago but we never wanted you or your siblings to be in danger of getting hurt. We knew if they couldn't kill us, they would come after you and we weren't going to let that happen. So that's why you never met your relatives until you started college. I didn't want you to have anything to do with them and I hope you can understand why now that I've told you everything." Katrina replied.

"Yes ma'am, I understand better than I did before. Had I known, I would have never gone to Uncle Walter's church or let him help me with anything. I am so disgusted by what they let happen. So Mama is what Earnest said about them doing porn videos and having a strip club true?" Jamaal asked.

"Yeah, that's true." Katrina said.

"But they never showed us that part of everything. But when Earnest described the building to me, I realized that Ramon and I walked past it. But they never told us what it was." Jamaal said.

"Yeah, they were probably going to wait until you were both in a few months and then open you up to it. I'm just glad Ramon ended up leaving like he did and that we're talking about this now because you're not going to be taken over any further by this! You remember when you were about to graduate from high school and I told you that a breaking of day would come?" Katrina asked.

"Yes ma'am, I remember. I never knew what you meant by that but you told me I would one day find out." Jamaal replied.

"I did and it's about to happen. That's part of why your aunt and I are here." Katrina said.

"So you're going to expose Uncle Walter and the church by yourself? I mean, I'll come with you but it's only three of us! Maybe four if Earnest will come." Jamaal said.

"Earnest is aware of what we're planning to do and he wants to come but he's still recovering from his injuries so I told him we could come see him after everything was done." Tracy said.

"Okay so it's just the three of us then?" Jamaal asked.

"Oh no, it won't just be the three of us. We went to one of the local news stations here and we told them everything we know and even showed them proof that we had to keep buried for all these years out of fear of what would happen to us for speaking out." Katrina replied.

"WOW! Mama, the news is getting involved?" Jamaal asked in shock.

"Yes they are. The news anchor I spoke to just text me back and she said they're ready for us. They're going to meet us at the church and they sent another anchor and a camera crew to their secret location to bust that up live and in person! It's going to be great but we need to get going. Are you ready?" Katrina asked.

"I'm ready Mama but shouldn't the police be meeting us there too?" Jamaal asked as Katrina and Tracy glanced at each other.

"They should but they're not, at least not right now. It's going to happen when this story breaks though and when it happens, they will be arresting some of their own officers for engaging in the illegal mess with them." Katrina said.

"Wow, the police are in on this too Mama?" he asked, surprised.

"Yeah, some of them are. But we have what we need to take all of this down and expose this messy church for the snakes they really are! So are you ready, Jamaal?" Katrina asked as Jamaal smiled.

"Yeah Mama, I'm ready. Let's do this! It's time for Day to break!" Jamaal said as he, Katrina and Tracy hugged each other again before leaving the hotel.

ONE MONTH LATER

Jamaal Day was able to witness his mother and aunt take a bold stand that many people who have been damaged by the church were too afraid to take. Jamaal was pulled into the trap of many by his pastor who sold him a false hope and convinced him to do whatever it took to cover his pastor. But when Jamaal's loyalty to his pastor was tested against what is right and wrong, Jamaal chose to do what was right so that his mother and his aunt could experience a level of freedom and healing by speaking up and being a voice for so many people who were afraid to break their silence. The exposing of Walter's church turned up ten young women who had been kidnapped by Walter and several of his other leaders and locked away in cages and sold for the night to older men who wanted to pay for sex between the ages of sixteen and nineteen who were reported missing by family. Several more young women who were former members came forward to report being raped and sexually assaulted by Walter, Calvin, Preston and other ministers at Walter's church.

Jamaal moved back to Miami and decided to attend college closer to home after what took place at Walter's church. Other leaders in the area made attempts to invite Jamaal and his family to their church but they didn't accept the offer. Deep down, Jamaal wanted to connect with a local church he was invited to by one of his friends on campus but he knew his mom and aunt would never agree to it after what took place exposing Walter's church. They were convinced that no pastor and no church could be trusted. Jamaal moved back home agreeing to never attend church again but after meeting students on campus who truly did love God, Jamaal could feel something inside of him that wanted to seek God and not allow what happened to change his heart. But he felt conflicted between what he was feeling and what he agreed to do for his mom and his family. Jamaal couldn't deal with the pressure of such a tough decision and decided not to take the risk of being hurt again by choosing to focus on school and working part-time with Earnest at the bank. As great as it was to see the church who dishonored God be exposed, seeing the aftermath of Walter and the other leaders' actions is heartbreaking.

It's moments like this that tend to push people even further away from God instead of closer to him. Jamaal, Katrina and Tracy are representatives of many who have been damaged by the actions of leaders as well people inside the four walls of the church. The prayer of those who are truly a part of the church of God should be for the hearts of people like them to find their way back to God and His love so that their heart towards Him won't turn cold.